The Long Dinner

By

H. C. Bailey

British Library Cataloguing-in-Publication Data
A catalogue record for this book is available from
the British Library

Contents

H. C. BAILEY

Henry Christopher Bailey was born in London in 1878. In his youth he attended the City of London School, before graduating with a degree in classics from the University of Oxford. Between 1901 and 1946, he worked for the *Daily Telegraph*, first as a drama critic, then as a war correspondent, and finally as an editorialist. During this time, Bailey spent his evenings writing, and became a popular author of detective fiction. He created two series; the first featuring Reggie Fortune, a medicine expert employed by Scotland Yard, and the second featuring Joshua Clunk, a solicitor for lower class criminals. Bailey was prolific, and Fortune featured in no less than twelve collections of short stories between 1920 and 1940. Clunk, meanwhile, appears in eleven novels published between 1930 and 1950, including *The Sullen Sky Mystery* (1935), widely regarded as Bailey's *magnum opus*. Bailey died in Llanfairfechen, North Wales.

THE LONG DINNER

H. C. Bailey

'I dislike you,' said Mr Fortune. 'Some of the dirtiest linen I've seen.' He gazed morosely at the Chief of the Criminal Investigation Department.

'Quite,' Lomas agreed. 'Dirty fellow. What about those stains?'

'Oh, my dear chap!' Mr Fortune mourned. 'Paint. All sorts of paint. Also food and drink and assorted filth. Why worry me? What did you expect? Human gore?'

'I had no expectations,' said Lomas sweetly.

A certain intensity came into Mr Fortune's blue eyes. 'Yes. I hate you,' he murmured. 'Anything else you wanted to know?'

'A lot of things,' Lomas said. 'You're not useful, Reginald. I want to know what sort of fellow he was, and what's become of him.'

'He was an artist of dark complexion. He painted both in oils and water-colours. He lived a coarse and dissolute life, and had expensive tastes. What's become of him, I haven't the slightest idea. I should say he was on the way to the devil. What's it all about? Why this interest in the debauched artist?'

'Because the fellow's vanished,' said Lomas. 'He is a painter of sorts, as you say. Name—Derry Farquhar. He had a talent and a bit of success years ago, and he's gone downhill ever since. Not

3

altogether unknown to the police—money under false pretences and that sort of thing—but never any clear case. Ten days ago a woman turned up to give information that Mr Derry Farquhar was missing. He had some money out of her—a matter of fifty pounds—three months ago. She don't complain of that. She was used to handing him donations—that kind of woman and that kind of man. What worries her is that, since this particular fifty pounds, he's faded out. And it is a queer case. He's lived these ten years in a rat-hole of a flat in Bloomsbury. He's not been seen there for months. That's unlike him. He's never been long away before. A regular London loafer. And his own money—he's got a little income from a trust—has piled up in the bank. August and September dividends untouched. That's absolutely unlike him. Besides that: one night about a fortnight ago—we can't fix the date—somebody was heard in the flat making a good deal of noise. When Bell went to have a look at things, he found the place in a devil of a mess, and a heap of foul linen. So we sent that to you.'

'Hoping for proof of bloodshed,' Reggie murmured. 'Hopeful fellow. Shirts extremely foul, but affordin' no evidence of foul play. Blood is absent. Almost the only substance that is.'

'So you don't believe there's anything in the case?'

'My dear chap! Oh, my dear chap,' Reggie opened large, plaintive eyes. 'Belief is a serious operation. I believe you haven't found anything. That's all. I should say you didn't look.'

'Thank you,' said Lomas acidly. 'Bell raked it all over' He spoke into the telephone, and Superintendent Bell arrived with a fat folder.

'Mr Fortune thinks you've missed something, Bell,' Lomas smiled.

'If there was anything any use, I have,' Bell said heavily. 'I'll be glad to hear what it is. Here's some photographs of the place, sir. And an inventory.'

'You might pick up a bargain, Reginald,' said Lomas, while Reggie, with a decent solemnity, perused the inventory and contemplated the photographs.

'Four oil paintings, fifteen water-colours. Unframed,' he read, and lifted a gaze of innocent enquiry to Bell.

'I'd call 'em clever, myself,' said Bell. 'Not nice, you know, but very bright and showy. Nudes of ladies, and that sort of thing. I should have thought he could have made a tidy living out of them. But a picture dealer that's seen 'em priced 'em at half a dollar each. Slick rubbish, he called 'em. I'm no hand at art. Anyway—it don't tell us anything.'

'I wouldn't say that. No,' Reggie murmured. 'Builds up the

character of Mr Farquhar for us. Person of no honour, even in his pot-boilin' art. However. Nothing else in the flat?'

'Some letters—mostly bills and duns. Nothing to show what he was up to. Nothing to work on.'

Reggie turned over the correspondence quickly. 'Yes. As you say.' He stopped at a crumpled, stained card. 'Where was this?'

'In a pocket of a dirty old sports coat,' Bell said. 'It's only a menu. I don't know why he kept it. Some faces drawn on the back. Perhaps he fancied 'em. No accounting for taste. Looks like drawing devils to me.'

'Rather diabolical, yes,' Reggie murmurd. 'Conventional devil. Mephistopheles in a flick.' The faces were sketched, in pencil, with a few accomplished strokes, but had no distinction: the same face in variations of grin and scowl and leer: a face of black brows, moustache, and pointed beard. 'Clever craftsman. Only clever.' He turned the card to the menu written on the front. 'My only aunt!' he moaned, and, in a hushed voice of awe read out:

DÎNER
Artichauts à l'Huile
Pommes de Terre à l'Huile
Porc frais froid aux Cornichons
Langouste Mayonnaise
Canard aux Navets
Omelette Rognons
Filet garni
Fromage à la Crème
Fruits, Biscuits

'Good Gad! Some dinner,' Lomas chuckled.

'I don't say I get it all,' Bell frowned. 'But what's it come to? He did himself well some time.'

'Well!' Reggie groaned. 'Oh, my dear chap! Artichokes in oil, cold pork, lobster, duck and turnips—and a kidney omelette and roast beef and trimmings.'

'I've got to own it wants a stomach,' said Bell gloomily. 'What then?'

'Died of indigestion,' said Lomas. 'Or committed suicide in the pangs. Very natural. Very just. There you are, Bell. Mr Fortune has solved the case.'

'I was taking it seriously myself,' Bell glowered at them.

'Oh, my Bell!' Reggie sighed. 'So was I.' He turned on Lomas. 'Incurably flippant mind, your mind. This is the essential fact. Look for Mr Farquhar in Brittany.'

Bell breathed hard. 'How do you get to that, sir?'

5

'No place but a Brittany inn ever served such a dinner.'

Bell rubbed his chin. 'I see. I don't know Brittany myelf, I'm glad to say. I got to own I never met a dinner like it.' He looked at Lomas. 'That means putting it back on the French.'

'Quite,' Lomas smiled. 'Brilliant thought, Reginald. Would you be surprised to hear that Paris is asking us to look for Mr Derry Farquhar in England?'

'Well, well,' Reggie surveyed him with patient contempt. 'Another relevant fact which you didn't mention. Also indicatin' an association of your Mr Farquhar with France.'

'If you like,' Lomas shrugged. 'But the point is they are sure he's here. Dubois is coming over today. I'm taking him to dine at the club. You'd better join us.'

'Oh, no. No,' Reggie said quickly. 'Dubois will dine with me. You bring him along. Your club dinner would destroy his faith in the English intelligence. If any. And I like Dubois. Pleasant to discuss the case with a serious mind. Good-bye. Half past eight.' . . .

With a superior English smile, Lomas sat back and watched Reggie and Dubois consume that fantasia on pancakes, Crêpes Joan, which Reggie invented as an expression of the way of his wife with her husband. . . .

Dubois wiped his flowing moustaches. 'My homage,' he said reverently.

By way of a devilled biscuit, they came to another claret. Dubois looked and smelt and tasted, and his eyes returned thanks. 'Try it with a medlar,' Reggie purred.

'You are right. There is no fruit better with wine.'

They engaged upon a ritual of ecstasy while Lomas gave himself a glass of port and lit a cigarette. At that, Reggie gave a reproachful stare. 'My only aunt! Forgive him, Dubois. He's mere modern English.'

'I pity profoundly,' Dubois sighed. 'A bleak life. This is a great wine, my friend. Of Pauillac, I think, eh? Of the last century?'

'Quite good, yes,' Reggie purred. 'Mouton Rothschild 1900.'

Dubois's large face beamed. 'Aha. Not so bad for poor old Dubois.'

They proceeded to a duet on claret. . . .

Lomas became restive. 'This unanimity is touching. Now you've embraced each other all over, we might come to business and see if you can keep it up.'

Dubois turned to him with a gesture of deprecation. 'Pardon, my friend. Have no fear. We agree always. But I will not delay you. The affair is, after all, very simple—'

'Quite,' Lomas smiled. 'Tell Fortune. He has his own ideas about it.'

'Aha,' Dubois's eyebrows went up. 'I shall be grateful. Well, I begin, then, with Max Weber. He is what you call a profiteer, but, after all, a good fellow. It is a year ago he married a pretty lady. She was by courtesy an actress, the beautiful Clotilde. One has nothing else against her. They live together very happily in an apartment of luxury. Two weeks ago, they find that some of her jewels, which she had in her bedroom, are gone. Not all that Weber had given her, the most valuable are at the bank, but diamonds worth five hundred thousand francs. Weber comes to the Sûreté and makes a complaint. What do we find? The servants, they have been with Weber many years, they are spoilt, they are careless; but dishonest—I think not. There is no sign of a burglary. But the day before the jewels were missed a man came to the Weber apartment who asked for Madame Weber and was told she was not at home. That was true in fact, but, also, Weber's man did not like his look. A *gouape* of the finest water—that is the description. What you call a blackguard, is it not? The man was shabby but showy; he resembled exactly a loafer in the Quartier Latin, an artist *décavé*—how do you say that.'

'On his uppers. Yes. Still more interesting. But not an identification, Dubois.'

'Be patient still. You see—here is a type which might well have known *la belle* Clotilde before she was Madame Weber. Very well. This gentleman, when he was refused at the Weber door, he did not go far away. We have a *concierge* who saw him loitering till the afternoon at least. In the afternoon the Weber servants take their ease. The man went to a *café*—he admits it—one woman calls on a friend here, another there. What more easy than for the blackguard artist to enter, to take the jewel case, to hop it, as you say.'

'We do. Yes.'

'Well, then, I begin from a description of Monsieur the Blackguard. It is not so bad. A man who is plump and dark, with little dark whiskers, who has front teeth which stand out, who walks like a bird running, with short steps that go pit pat. He speaks French well enough, but not like a Frenchman. He wears clothes of orange colour, cut very loose, and a soft black hat of wide brim. Then I find that a man like this got into the night train from the Gare St Lazare for Dieppe—that is, you see, to come back to England by the cheap way. Very well. We have worked in the Quartier Latin, we find that a man like this was seen a day or two in some of the cafés. They remember him well, because they knew him ten years ago when he was a student. They are like that, these old folks of the Quartier—it pays. Then his name was Farquhar, Derek Farquhar, an Englishman.' Dubois twirled his moustaches. 'So you see, my friend, I dare to trouble Mr Lomas to find me in England this Farquhar.'

'Yes. Method quite sound,' Reggie mumbled. 'As a method.'

'My poor Reginald,' Lomas laughed. 'What a mournful, reluctant confession! You've hurt him, Dubois. He was quite sure Mr Farquhar was traversing the wilds of Brittany.'

'Aha,' Dubois put up his eyebrows, and made a gesture of respect to Reggie. 'My dear friend, never I consult you but I find you see farther than I. Tell me then.'

'Oh, no. No. Don't see it all,' Reggie mumbled, and told him of the menu of the long dinner.

'Without doubt that dinner was served in Brittany,' Dubois nodded. 'I agree, it is probable he had been there not so long ago. But what of that? He was a painter, he had studied in France, and Brittany is always full of painters.'

'Yes. You're neglectin' part of the evidence. Faces on the back of the menu.' He took out his pocketbook, and sketched the black-browed, black-bearded countenance. 'Like that.'

'The devil,' said Dubois.

'As you say. Devil of opera and fancy ball. The ordinary Mephistopheles. Associated by your Mr Farquhar with Brittany.'

'My dear Fortune!' Dubois's big face twisted into a quizzical smile. 'You are very subtle. Me, I find this is to make too much of little things. After all, drawing devils, it is common sport—you find devils all over our comic papers—a devil and a pretty lady—and he drew pretty ladies often, you say, this Farquhar—and this is a very common devil.'

'Yes, rational criticism,' Reggie murmured, looking at him with dreamy eyes. 'You're very rational, Dubois. However. Any association of the Webers with Brittany?'

'Oh, my friend!' Dubois smiled indulgently. 'None at all. And when they go out of Paris, it is to Monte Carlo, to Aix, not to rough it in Brittany, you may be sure. No. You shall forgive me, but I find nothing in your menu to change my mind. I must look for my Farquhar here.' He shook his head sadly at Reggie. 'I am desolated that you do not agree.' He turned to Lomas. 'But this is the only way, hein?'

'Absolutely. There's no other line at all,' said Lomas, with satisfaction. 'Don't let Fortune worry you. He lives to see what isn't there. Wonderful imagination.'

'My only aunt!' Reggie moaned. 'Not me, no. No imagination at all. Only simple faith in facts. You people ignore 'em when they're not rational. Unscientific and superstitious. However. Let's pretend and see what we get. Go your own way.'

'One does as one can,' Dubois shrugged.

'Quite. Fortune is never content with the possible. We must work it out here. I've put things in train for you. We have a copy of Farquhar's photograph. That's been circulated with description, and there's a general warning out for him and the jewels. We're combing out all his friends and his usual haunts.'

' "So runs my dream, but what am I?" ' Reggie murmured. ' "An infant cryin' in the night. An infant cryin' for the light—" Well, well. Are we downhearted? Yes. A little Armagnac would be grateful and comfortin'.' He turned the conversation imperatively to the qualities of that liqueur, and Dubois was quick with respectful responses. Lomas relapsed upon Olympian disdain and whisky and soda.

When he took Dubois away, 'Fantastic fellow, Fortune, isn't he?' Lomas smiled. 'Mind of the first order, but never content to use it.'

'An artist, my friend,' said Dubois. 'A great artist. He feels life. We think about it.'

'Damme, you don't believe he's right about this Brittany guess?'

'What do I know?' Dubois shrugged. 'It means nothing. Therefore it is nothing for us. However, one must confess, he is disconcerting, your Mr Fortune. He makes one always doubt.'

This, when he heard of it, Reggie considered the greatest compliment which he ever had, except from his wife. He also thinks it deserved. . . .

Some days later he was engaged upon the production in his marionette theatre of the tragedy of *Don Juan*, lyrics by Lord Byron, prose and music by Mr Fortune, when the telephone called him from a poignant passage on the rejection of his hero by hell.

'Yes, Fortune speaking. "Between two worlds life hovers like a star." Perhaps you didn't know that, Lomas. "How little do we know that which we are." Discovery of the late Lord Byron. I'm settin' it to music. Departmental ditty for the Criminal Investigation Department. I—'

'Could you listen for a moment?' said Lomas sweetly. 'You might be interested.'

'Not likely, no. However. What's worryin' you?'

'Nothing, except sympathy for you, Reginald. I'm afraid you'll suffer. To break it gently, we've traced Farquhar. But not in Brittany, Reginald.'

Reggie remained calm. 'No. Of course not,' he moaned. 'You weren't trying. I don't want to hear what you've missed. Takes too long.'

A sound of mockery came over the wire. 'Are you ever wrong, Reginald? No. It's always the other fellow. But the awkward fact is, Farquhar hadn't gone to Brittany, he'd gone to Westshire. So that was the only place we could find him. We have our limitations.'

'You have. Yes. *C'est brutal, mais ça marche.* You're clumsy, but you move—sometimes—like the early cars. What has he got to say for himself?'

'I don't know. We haven't put our hands on him yet. We—what?'

'Pardon me. It was only emotion. A sob of reverence. Oh, my Lomas. You found the only place you could find him, so you haven't found him. The perfect official. No results, but always the superior person.'

'Results quite satisfactory,' Lomas snapped. 'We had a clear identification. He's been staying at Lyncombe. He's bolted again. No doubt found we were on his track. But we shall get him. They're combing out the district. Bell's gone down with Dubois.'

'Splendid. Always shut the stable door when the horse has been removed. I'll go too. I like watching that operation. Raises my confidence in the police force.' . . .

As the moon rose over the sea, Reggie's car drove into Lyncombe. It is a holiday town of some luxury. The affronts to nature of its blocks of hotel and twisting roads of villas for the opulent retired have not yet been able to spoil all the beauty of cliff and cove.

When Reggie saw it, the banal buildings and the headlands were mingled in moonlight to make a dreamland, and the sea was a black mystery with a glittering path on it.

He went to the newest hotel, he bathed well and dined badly, and, as he sat smoking his consolatory pipe on a balcony where the soft air smelt of chrysanthemums and the sea, Dubois came to him with Bell.

'Aha.' Dubois spoke. 'You have not gone to Brittany then, my friend?'

'No. No. Followin' the higher intelligence. I have a humble mind. And where have you got to?'

'We have got to the tracks of Farquhar, there is no doubt of that. What is remarkable, he had registered in his own name at the hotel, and the people there they recognise his photograph—they are sure of it. In fact, it is a face to be sure of, a rabbit face.'

'The identification's all right,' Bell grunted. 'The devil of it is, he's gone again, Mr Fortune. He went in a hurry too. Left all his traps behind, such as they were. The hotel people think he was just bilking them. He'd been a matter of ten days and not paid anything, and his baggage is worth about nothing—a battered old suitcase and some duds fit for the dust-bin.'

'Oh, Peter!' Reggie moaned. 'No, Bell, no. I haven't got to look at his shirts again?'

'I'm not asking you, sir. There's no sort of reason to think there was anything done to him. He just went out and didn't come back. Three days ago. I don't see any light at all. What he was doing here, beats me. You can say he was hiding with the swag he got in Paris. But then, why did he register in his own name? Say he was just a silly ass—you do get that kind of amateur thief. But what has he bolted for? He couldn't have had any suspicions we were on to him. We weren't, at the time he faded out.'

'But, my friend, you go too fast,' said Dubois. 'From you, no, he could not have had any alarm. But there is the other end—Paris. It is very possible that a friend in Paris warned him the police were searching for him.'

'All right,' Bell grunted. 'I give you that. Why would he make the hotel people notice him by bolting without paying his bill? Silly again. Sheer silly. He'd got a pot of money, if he did have the jewels, like you say. Going off without paying 'em just sent them to inform the police quick.'

'That is well argued. You have an insight, a power of mind, my friend.' Dubois's voice was silky. 'But what have we then? It is quite natural that Farquhar should disappear again, it is not natural that he should disappear like this. For me, I confess I do not find myself able to form an idea of Farquhar. That he is the type to rob such a woman as Clotilde, there is evidence enough—he had the knowledge, he had the opportunity. So far, there are a thousand cases like it. But that he should then retire to such a paradise of the bourgeois, that is not like his type at all.'

'That's right,' said Bell. 'No sense in it anyway.'

'No. As you say,' Reggie murmured. 'That struck me. Happy to agree with everybody. We don't know anything about anything.'

'Bigre! You go a little strong,' Dubois rumbled. 'Come, there is at least a connection with Clotilde, and her jewels are gone. Be sure of that. Weber is an honest man—except in business. And what, now, is your hypothesis? You said look for him in Brittany. This at least is certain—he had not gone there. What the devil should he have to do with this so correct Lyncombe? As much as with our rough Brittany.'

'Yes. Quite obscure. I haven't the slightest idea what he's been doing. However. Are we downhearted? No. We're in touch with the fundamental problem now. Why does Mr Farquhar deal with Brittany and Clotilde and Lyncombe? First method of solution clearly indicated. Find out what he did do in Lyncombe. That ought to be an easy one, Bell. He must have been noticed. He'd be conspicuous in this correct place. Good night.'

The next day he sat upon the same balcony, spreading the first scone of his tea with clotted cream and blackberry jelly, when the two returned.

'What! Have you not moved since last night?' Dubois made a grimace at him.

'My dear chap! Just walked all along one of the bays. And back. Great big bay. Exercise demanded by impatient and fretful brain. Rest is better. Have a splitter. They're too heavy. But the cream is sound.'

Dubois shuddered. 'Brr! You are a wonderful animal. Me, I am only human. But Bell has news for you. Tell him, old fellow.'

'It's like this,' Bell explained. 'About a week ago—that's three or four days before he disappeared, we can't fix the date nearer—Farquhar went to call at one of the big houses here. There's no doubt about that. It's rather like the Paris case. He was seen loafing round before and after—as you said, he's the sort of chap to get noticed. The house he went to belongs to an old gentleman—Mr Lane Hudson. Lived here for years. Very rich, they say. Made his money in South Wales, and came here when he retired. Well, he's eighty or more; he's half paralysed—only gets about his house and grounds in a wheeled chair. I've seen him; I've had a talk with him. His mind's all right. He looks like a mummy, only a bit plumped out. Sort of yellow, leathery face that don't change or move. Sits in his chair looking at nothing, and talks soft and thick. He tells me he never heard of Farquhar: didn't so much as know Farquhar had been to his house: that's quite in order, it's his rule that the servants tell anybody not known he's not well enough to see people, and I don't blame him. I wouldn't want strangers to come and look at me if I was like he is. I gave him an idea of the sort of fellow Farquhar was, and watched him pretty close, but he didn't turn a hair. He just said again he had no knowledge of any such person, and I believe him. He wasn't interested. He told me the fellow had no doubt come begging for money; he was much exposed to that sort of thing—we ought to stop it—and good day Mr Superintendent. Anyhow, it's certain Farquhar didn't see him. The old butler and the nurse bear that out, and they never heard of Farquhar before. The butler saw him and turned him away—had a spot of bother over it, but didn't worry. Like the old man, he says they do have impudent beggars now and then. So here's another nice old dead end.'

'Yes. As you say. Rather weird isn't it? The flamboyant

debauched Farquhar knockin' at the door—to get to a paralysed old rich man who never heard of him. I wonder. Curious selection of people to call on by our Mr Farquhar. A pretty lady of Paris who's married money and settled down on it; a rich old Welshman who's helpless on the edge of the grave. And neither of 'em sees Mr Farquhar—accordin' to the evidence—neither will admit to knowin' anything about him. Very odd. Yes.' Reggie turned large, melancholy eyes on Dubois. 'Takes your fancy, what? The black-guard artist knockin', knockin', and, upstairs, a mummy of a man helpless in his chair.'

'Name of a name!' Dubois rumbled. 'It is fantasy pure. One sees such things in dreams. This has no more meaning.'

'No. Not to us. But it happened. Therefore it had a cause. Mr Lane Hudson lives all alone, what—except for servants?'

'That's right, sir,' Bell nodded. 'He's been a widower this long time. Only one child—daughter—and there's a grandson, quite a kid. Daughter's been married twice—first to a chap called Tracy, now to a Mr Bernal—son by the first marriage, no other children.'

'You have taken pains, Bell,' Reggie smiled.

'Well, I got everything I could think of,' said Bell, with gloomy satisfaction. 'Not knowing what I wanted. And there's nothing I do want in what I've got. The Bernals come here fairly regular—Mr and Mrs Bernal, not the child—they've been staying with the old man just now. Usual autumn visit. They were there when Far-quhar called, and after—didn't go away till last Wednesday; that's before Farquhar disappeared, you see, the day before. Farquhar didn't ask for the Bernals, and they didn't see him at all, the servants say. So there you are. The Bernals don't link up any way. That peters out, like everything else.'

'Yes. Taken a lot of pains,' Reggie murmured.

'What would you have?' Dubois shrugged. 'To amass useless knowledge—it is our only method; one is condemned to it. Ours is a slow trade, my friend. We gather facts and facts and facts, and so, if we are lucky, eliminate ninety-nine of the hundred and use, at last, one.'

'Yes. As you say,' Reggie mumbled. 'Where do the Bernals live, Bell?'

'In France, sir,' said Bell, and Reggie opened his eyes.

'Aha!' Dubois made a grimace, and pointed a broad finger at him. 'There, my friend. The one grand fact, is it not? In France! And Brittany is in France! But alas, my dear Fortune, they do not live in Brittany! Far from it. They live in the south, near Cannes; they have lived there—what do I know?—since they were married, *hein*?' he turned to Bell.

'That's right,' Bell grunted. 'Lady set up house there with her first husband. He had to live in the south of France—gassed in the war.'

'You see?' Dubois smiled. 'It is still the useless knowledge. And your vision of Brittany, my friend, it has no substance still.'

'I wonder,' Reggie mumbled, and sank deep in his chair. . . .

He is, even without hope, conscientious. That night he examined another set of Farquhar's dirty linen, but neither in that nor the rest of the worthless luggage found any information. Prodded by him, Bell enquired of the Hudson household where the Bernals were to be found, but could obtain only the address of their Cannes villa, for they were reported to be going back by car. Dubois was persuaded to telegraph Cannes and received the reply that the Bernal villa was shut up; monsieur and madame were away motoring, and their boy at school—what school nobody knew.

'Then what?' Dubois summed up. 'Nothing to do.'

'Not tonight, no,' Reggie yawned. 'I'm going to bed.'

'To dream of Brittany, *hein*?'

'I never dream,' said Reggie, with indignation. . . .

But he was waked in the night. He rubbed his eyes and looked up to see Dubois's large face above him. 'Oh, my hat,' he moaned. 'What is it? Why won't it wait?'

'Courage, my friend. They have found him. At least, they think so. Some fishermen, going out yesterday evening, they found a body on the rocks at what they call Granny's Cove. Come. The brave Bell wants you to see.'

'Bless him,' Reggie groaned, and rolled out of bed. 'What is life that one should seek it? I ask you.' And, slipping clothes on him, swiftly he crooned, ' "Three fishers went sailin' out into the west, out into the west, as the sun went down"—and incredibly caught the incredible Farquhar.'

'You are right,' Dubois nodded. 'Nothing clear, nothing sure. The more it changes, the more it is the same, this accursed case. It has no shape; there is no reason in it.'

'Structure not yet determined. No,' Reggie mumbled, parting his hair, for he will always be neat. 'We're not bein' very clever. Ought to be able to describe the whole thing from available evidence of its existence. Same like inferrin' the age of reptiles from a fossil or two—"dragons of the prime, tearin' each other in the slime, were mellow music unto him." Yes. The struggle for life of the reptiles might be mellow music compared to the diversions of Mr Farquhar and friends. Progressive world, Dubois.'

'Name of a dog!' Dubois exclaimed. 'When you are philosophic, my stomach turns over. What is in your mind?'

'Feelin' of impotence. Very uncomfortable,' Reggie moaned, and muffled himself to the chin and made haste out.

In the mortuary Bell introduced them to a body covered by a sheet. 'Here you are, sir.' He stepped aside. 'The clothes seem to be Farquhar's clothes all right. Sort of orange tweed and green flannel trousers. But I don't know about the man.'

Reggie drew back the sheet from what was left of a face.

'*Saprelotte!*' Dubois rumbled. 'The fish have bitten.'

'Well, I leave it to you,' said Bell thickly. . . .

Under a sunlit breeze the sea was dancing bright, the mists flying inland from the valleys to the dim bank of the moor, when Reggie came out again.

He drove back to his hotel, and shaved and bathed and rang up the police station. Bell and Dubois arrived to find him in his room, eating with appetite grilled ham and buttered eggs.

'My envy; all my envy,' Dubois pulled a face. 'This is greatness. The English genius at the highest.'

'Oh, no. No,' Reggie protested. 'Natural man. Well. The corpse is that of Mr Farquhar as per invoice. Prominent teeth not impaired by activities of the lobsters. Some other contours still visible. The marmalade—thanks. Yes. Hair, colourin', size and so forth agree. Mr Farquhar's been in the sea three or four days. Correspondin' with date of disappearance. Cause of death, drowning. Severe contusions on head and body, inflicted before death. Possibly by blows, possibly by fall. Might have fallen from cliff; might have been dashed on rocks by sea. No certainty to be obtained. That's the medical evidence.'

'You are talking!' Dubois exclaimed. '*Flute!* There we are again. Whatever arrives, it will mean nothing for us. Here is murder, suicide, accident—what you please.'

'I wonder.' Reggie began to peel an apple. 'Anything in his pockets, Bell?'

'A lot of money, sir. Nothing else. The notes are all sodden, but it's a good wad, and some are fifties. Might be five or six hundred pounds. So he wasn't robbed.'

'And then?' said Dubois. 'It is not enough for all the jewels of Clotilde, but it is something in hand. Will you tell me what the devil he was doing at the door of this paralysed millionaire? It means nothing, none of it.'

'No. Still amassin' useless knowledge, as you were sayin'.' Reggie gazed at Dubois with dreamy eyes. 'I should say that's what we came here for. Don't seem the right place, does it? However. As we are here, let's try and get a little more before departure. Usin' the local talent. Bell—your fishermen—have they got any ideas

15

where a fellow would tumble into the sea to be washed up into Granny's Cove?'

'Ah.' Bell was pleased. 'I have been asking about that, sir. Supposing he got in from the land, they think it would be somewhere round by Shag Nose. That's a bit o' cliff west o' the town. I'm having men search round and enquire. But the scent's pretty cold by now.'

'Yes. As you say,' Reggie sighed. His eyes grew large and melancholy. 'Is it far?' he said, in a voice of fear.

'Matter of a mile or two.'

'Oh, my Bell.' Reggie groaned. He pushed back his chair. He rose stiffly. 'Come on.'

Shag Nose is a headland from which dark cliffs fall sheer. Below them stretches seaward a ridge of rocks, which stand bare some way out at low tide, and in the flood make a turmoil of eddies and broken water.

The top of the headland is a flat of springy turf, in which are many tufts of thrift and cushions of stunted gorse.

'Brr. It is bleak,' Dubois complained. 'Will you tell me why Farquhar should come here? He was not—how do you say?—a man for the great open spaces.'

'Know the answer, don't you?' Reggie mumbled.

'Perfectly. He came to meet somebody in secret who desired to make an end of him. Very well. But who then? Not the paralysed one. Not the son-in-law either. It is in evidence that the son-in-law was gone before Farquhar disappeared.'

'That's right. I verified that,' Bell grunted. 'Bernal and his wife left the night before.'

'There we are again,' Dubois shrugged. 'Nothing means anything. For certain, it is not a perfect alibi. They went by car; they could come back and not be seen. But it is an alibi that will stand unless you have luck, which you have not yet, my dear Bell, God knows.'

'Not an easy case. No,' Reggie murmured. 'However. Possibilities not yet examined. Lyncombe's on the coast. Had you noticed that? I wonder if any little boat from France came in while Farquhar was still alive.'

Dubois laughed. Dubois clapped him on the shoulder. 'Magnificent! How you are resolute, my friend. Always the great idea! A boat from Brittany, hein? That would solve everything. The good Farquhar was so kind as to come here and meet it and be killed by the brave Bretons. And the paralysed millionaire, he was merely a diversion to pass the time.'

'Yes. We are not amused,' Reggie moaned. 'You're in such a

hurry. Bell—what's the local talent say about the tide? When was high water on the night Farquhar disappeared?'

'Not till the early morning, sir. Tide was going out from about three in the afternoon onwards.'

'I see. At dusk and after, that reef o' rocks would be comin' out of the water. Assumin' he went over the cliff in the dark or twilight, he'd fall on the rocks.'

'That's right. Of course he might bounce into the sea. But I've got a man or two down there searching the shore and the cliff-side.'

'Good man.' Reggie smiled, and wandered away to the cliff edge.

'Yes. It is most correct,' Dubois shrugged. 'I should do it, I avow. But also I should expect nothing, nothing. After all, we are late. We arrive late at everything.'

Reggie turned and stared at him. 'I know. That's what I'm afraid of,' he mumbled.

He wandered to and fro about the ground near the cliff edge, and found nothing which satisfied him, and at last lay down on his stomach where a jutting of the headland gave him a view of the cliffs on either side.

Two men scrambled about over the rocks below, scanning the cliff face, prying into every crevice they could reach . . . one of them vanished under an overhanging ledge, appeared again, working round it, was lost in a cleft . . . when he came out he had something in his hand.

'Name of a pipe!' Dubois rumbled. 'Is it possible we have luck at last?'

'No.' Reggie stood up. 'Won't be luck, whatever it is. Reward of virtue. Bell's infinite capacity for takin' pains.' . . .

A breathless policeman reached the top of the cliff, and held out a sodden book. 'That's the only perishing thing there is down there, sir,' he panted. 'Not a trace of nothing else.'

Bell gave it to Reggie. It was a sketch-book of the size to slide into a man's pocket. The first leaf bore, in a flamboyant scrawl, the name Derek Farquhar.

'Ah. That fixes it, then,' said Bell. 'He did go over this cliff, and his sketch-book came out of his pocket as he bounced on the ledges.'

'Very well,' Dubois shrugged. 'We know now as much as we guessed. Which means nothing.'

Reggie sat down and began to separate the book's wet pages.

Farquhar had drawn, in pencil, notes rather than sketches at first, scraps of face and figure and scene which took his unholy fancy, a drunken girl, a nasty stage dance, variations of impropriety. Then came some parades of men and women bathing, not less unpleasant, but more studied. 'Aha! Here is something seen at least,' said Dubois.

'Yes, I think so,' Reggie murmured, and turned the page.

The next sketch showed children dancing—small boys and girls. Some touch of cruelty was in the drawing—they were made to look ungainly—but it had power; it gave them an intensity of frail life which was at once pathetic and grotesque. They danced round a giant statue—a block in which the shape of a woman was burlesqued, hideously fat and thin, with a flat, foolish face. There were no clothes on it, but rough lines which might be girdle and necklace.

'What the devil!' Dubois exclaimed. 'This is an oddity. He discovers he had a talent, the animal.'

Reggie did not answer. For a moment more he gazed at the children and the statue, and he shivered, then he turned the other pages of the book. There were some notes of faces, then several satires on the respectability of Lyncombe—the sea front, with nymphs in Bath chairs propelled by satyrs and satyrs propelled by nymphs. He turned back to the dancing children and the giant female statue, and stared at it, and his round face was pale. 'Yes. Farquhar had talent,' he said. 'Played the devil with it all his life. And yet it works on the other side. What's the quickest way to Brittany? London and then Paris by air. Come on.'

Dubois swore by a paper bag and caught him up. 'What, then? How do you find your Brittany again in this?'

'The statue,' Reggie snapped. 'Sort of statue you see in Brittany. Nowhere else. He didn't invent that out of his dirty mind. He'd seen it. It meant something to him. I should say he'd seen the children too.'

'You go beyond me,' said Dubois. 'Well, it is not the first time. A statue of Brittany, eh? You mean the old things they have among the standing stones and the menhirs and dolmens. A primitive goddess. The devil! I do not see our Farquhar interested in antiquities. But it is the more striking that he studied her. I give you that. And the children? I will swear he was not a lover of children.'

'No. He wasn't. That came out in the drawing. Not a nice man. It pleased him to think of children dancin' round the barbarous female.'

'I believe you,' said Dubois. 'The devil was in that drawing.'

'Yes. Devilish feelin'. Yes. And yet it's going to help. Because the degenerate fellow had talent. Not wholly a bad world.'

'Optimist. Be it so. But what can you make the drawing mean, then?'

'I haven't the slightest idea,' Reggie mumbled. 'Place of child life in the career of the late Farquhar very obscure. Only trace yet discovered, the Bernals have a child. No inference justified. I'm going to Brittany. I'm goin' to look for traces round that statue. And meanwhile—Bell has to find out if a French boat has been in to Lyncombe—you'd better set your people findin' the Bernals—with child. Have the Webers got a child?'

'Ah, no.' Dubois laughed. 'The beautiful Clotilde, she is not that type.'

'Pity. However. You might let me have a look at the Webers as I go through Paris.'

'With all my heart,' said Dubois. 'You understand, my friend, you command me. I see nothing, nothing at all, but I put myself in your hand.' He made a grimace. 'In fact there is nothing else to do. It is an affair for inspiration. I never had any.'

'Nor me, no,' Reggie was indignant. 'My only aunt! Inspired! I am not! I believe in evidence. That's all. You experts are so superior.' . . .

Next morning they sat in the *salon* of the Webers. It was overwhelming with the worst magnificence of the Second Empire—mirrors and gilding, marble and malachite and lapis lazuli. But the Webers, entering affectionately arm in arm, were only magnificent in their opulent proportions. Clotilde, a dark full-blown creature, had nothing more than powder on her face, no jewels but a string of pearls, and the exuberance of her shape was modified by a simple black dress. Weber's clumsy bulk was all in black too.

They welcomed Dubois with open arms; they talked together. What had he to tell them? They had heard that the cursed Farquhar had been discovered dead in England—it was staggering; had anything been found of the jewels?

Nothing, in effect, Dubois told them. Only, Farquhar had more money than such an animal ought to have. It was a pity.

Clotilde threw up her hands. Weber scolded.

Dubois regretted—but what to do? They must admit one had been quick, very quick, to trace Farquhar. They would certainly compliment his *confrère* from England—that produced perfunctory bows. What the English police asked—and they were right—it was could one learn anything of who had worked with Farquhar, why had he come to the apartment Weber?

The Webers were contemptuous. What use to ask such a question? One had not an acquaintance with thieves. As to why he came, why he picked out them to rob—a thief must go where there was something to steal—and they—well, one was known a little. Weber smirked at his wife, and she smiled at him.

'For sure. Everyone knows monsieur—and madame.' Dubois bowed. 'But I seek something more.'

They stormed. It was not to be supposed they should know anything of such a down-at-heel.

'Oh, no. No,' said Reggie quickly. 'But in the world of business'—he looked at Weber—'in the world of the theatre'—he looked at Clotilde—'the fellow might have crossed your path, what?'

That was soothing. They agreed the thing was possible. How could one tell? They chattered of the detrimentals they remembered—to no purpose.

Under plaintive looks from Reggie, Dubois broke that off with a brusque departure. When they were outside—'Well, you have met them!' Dubois shrugged. 'And if they are anything which is not ordinary I did not see it.'

Reggie gazed at him with round reproachful eyes. 'They were in mourning,' he moaned. 'You never told me that. Were they in mourning when you saw 'em before?'

'But yes,' Dubois frowned. 'Yes, certainly. What is the matter? Did you think they had put on mourning for the animal Farquhar?'

'My dear chap! Oh, my dear chap,' Reggie sighed. 'Find out why they are in mourning. Quietly, quite quietly. Good-bye. Meet you at the station.' . . .

The night express to Nantes and Quimper drew out of Paris. They ate a grim and taciturn dinner. They went back to the sleeping car and shut themselves in Reggie's compartment. 'Well, I have done my work,' said Dubois. 'The Webers are in mourning for their nephew. A child of ten, whom Weber would have made his heir—his sister's son.'

'A child,' Reggie murmured. 'How did he die?'

'It was not in Brittany, my friend,' Dubois grinned. 'Besides it is not mysterious. He died at Fontainebleau, in August, of diphtheria. They had the best doctors of Paris. There you are again. It means nothing.'

'I wonder,' Reggie mumbled. 'Any news of the Bernals?'

'It appears they have passed through Touraine. If it is they, there was no child with them. Have no fear, they are watched for. One does not disappear in France.'

'You think not? Well, well. Remains the Bernal child. Not yet known to be dead. Of diphtheria or otherwise! I did a job o' work too. Talked to old Huet at the Institut. You know—the prehistoric man. He says Farquhar's goddess is the Woman of Sarn. Recognised her at once. She stands on about the last western hill in France. Weird sort o' place, Huet says. And he can't imagine why

Farquhar thought of children dancin' round her. The people are taught she's of the devil.'

'But you go on to see her?' Dubois made a grimace. 'The fixed idea.'

'No. Rational inference. Farquhar thought of her with children. And there's a child dead—and another child we can't find—belongin' to the people linked with Farquhar. I go on.'

'To the land's end—to the end of the world—and beyond. For your faith in yourself. My dear Fortune, you are sublime. Well, I follow you. Poor old Dubois. Sancho Panza to your Don Quixote, *hein?'* . . .

They came out of the train to a morning of soft sunshine and mellow ocean air. The twin spires of Quimper rose bright among their minarets, its sister rivers gleamed, and the wooded hill beyond glowed bronze. Dubois bustled away from breakfast to see officials. 'Don Quixote is a law to himself, but Sancho had better be correct, my friend.'

'Yes, rather,' Reggie mumbled, from a mouth full of honey. 'Conciliate the authorities. Liable to want 'em.'

'Always the optimist, my Quixote.'

'No. No. Only careful. Don't tell 'em anything.'

'Name of a name!' Dubois exploded. 'That is necessary, that warning. I have so much to tell!'

In an hour, they were driving away from Quimper, up over high moorland of heather and gorse and down again to a golden bay and a fishing village of many boats, then on westward, with glimpses of sea on either hand. There was never a tree, only, about the stone walls which divided the waves of bare land into a draught-board of little fields, thick growth of bramble and gorse. Beyond the next village, with its deep inlet of a harbour, the fields merged into moor again, and here and there rose giant stones, in line, in circle, and solitary.

'Brrr,' Dubois rumbled. 'Tombs or temples, what you please, it was a gaunt religion which put them up here on this windy end of the earth.'

The car stopped, the driver turned in his seat and pointed, and said he could drive no nearer, but that was the Woman of Sarn. 'She is lonely,' Dubois shrugged. 'There is no village near, my lad?'

'There is Sarn.' The driver pointed towards the southern sea. 'But it is nothing.'

Reggie plodded away through the heather. 'Well, this is hopeful, is it not?' Dubois caught him up. 'When we find her, what have we found? An idol in the desert. But you will go on to the end, my Quixote. Forward, then.'

21

They came to the statue, and stood, for its crude head rose high above theirs, looking up at it. 'And we have found it, one must avow,' Dubois shrugged. 'This is the lady Farquhar drew, devil a doubt. But, *saperlipopette*, she is worse here than on paper. She is real; she is a brute—all that there is of the beast in woman, emerging from the shapeless earth.'

'Inhuman and horrid human, yes,' Reggie murmured. 'Cruelty of life. Yes. He knew about that, the fellow who made her, poor beggar. So did Farquhar.'

'I believe it! But do you ask me to believe little children come and dance round this horror. Ah, no!'

'Oh, no. No. That never happened. Not in our time. Point of interest is, Farquhar thought it fittin' they should. Very interestin' point.' Reggie gave another look at the statue, and walked on towards the highest point of the moor.

From that he could see the tiny village of Sarn, huddled in a cove, the line of dark cliff, a long rampart against the Atlantic. Below the cliff top he made out a white house, of some size, which seemed to stand alone.

His face had a dreamy placidity as he came back to Dubois. 'Well, well. Not altogether desert,' he murmured. 'Something quite residential over there. Let's wander.'

They struck southward towards the sea. As they approached the white house, they saw that it was of modern pattern—concrete, in simple proportions, with more window than wall. Its site was well chosen, in a little hollow beneath the highest of the cliff, sheltered, yet high enough for a far prospect, taking all the southern sun.

'Of the new ugliness, eh?' said Dubois, whose taste is for elaboration in all things. 'All the last fads. It should be a sanatorium, not a house.'

'One of the possibilities, yes.' Reggie went on fast.

They came close above the house. It stood in a large walled enclosure, within which was a trim garden, but most of the space was taken by a paved yard with a roofed platform like a bandstand in the middle. Reggie stood still and surveyed it. Not a creature was to be seen. The acreage of window blazed blank and curtainless.

'The band is not playing.' Dubois made a grimace. 'It is not the season.'

Reggie did not answer. His eyes puckered to stare at a window within which the sun glinted on something of brass. He made a little inarticulate sound, and walked on, keeping above the house. But they saw no one, no sign of life, till they were close to the cliff edge.

Then a cove opened below them in a gleaming stretch of white shell sand, and on the sand children were playing: some of them at a happy-go-lucky game of rounders, some building castles, some tumbling over each other like puppies. On a rock sat, in placid guard over them, a man who had the black pointed beard, the heavy black brows, which Farquhar had sketched on his menu. But these Mephistophelean decorations did not display the leer and sneer of Farquhar's drawing. The owner watched the children with a grave and kindly attention which seemed to be interested in everyone. He called to them cheerily, and had gay answers. He laughed jovial satisfaction at their laughter.

Reggie took Dubois's arm and walked him away. 'Ah, my poor friend!' Dubois rumbled chuckles. 'There we are at last. We arrive. We have the brute goddess, we have the children, we have even the devil of our Farquhar. And behold! he is a genial paternal soul, and all the children love him. Oh, my poor friend!'

'Yes. Funny isn't it?' Reggie snapped. 'Dam' funny. Did you say the end? Then God forgive us. Which He wouldn't. He would not!'

Dubois gave him a queer look—something of derision, something of awe, and a good deal of doubt. 'When you talk like that'— a shrug, a wave of the hands—'it is outside reason, is it not? An inspiration of faith.'

'Faith that the world is reasonable. That's all,' Reggie snarled. 'Come on.'

'And where?'

'Down to this village.'

The huddled cottages of Sarn were already in sight. Then odours, a complex of stale fish and the filth of beast and man, could be smelt. Women clattered in sabots and laboured. Men lounged against the wall above the mess of the beach. A few small and ancient boats lay at anchor in the cove, and one of a larger size, and better condition, which had a motor engine.

They found a dirty *estaminet* and obtained from the landlord a bottle of nameless red wine. He said it was old, it was marvellous, but, being urged to share it, preferred a glass of the apple spirit, Calvados. 'Marvellous, it is the world,' Dubois grinned. 'You are altogether right. Calvados for us also, my friend. It is more humane.'

The landlord was slow of speech, and a pessimist. Even with several little glasses of Calvados inside him he would talk only of the hardness of life and the poverty of Sarn and the curse upon the modern sardine. Reggie agreed that life was dear and life was difficult, but, after all, they had still their good boats at Sarn— motor-boats indeed. The landlord denied it with gloomy vehemence: motors—not one—only in the *Badebec*, and that was no fishing-boat, that one. It was M. David's.

'Is it so?" Reggie yawned, and lit his pipe. He gazed dreamily down the village street to the hideous little church. From that— under a patched umbrella, to keep off the wind, which was high, or the sun, which was grown faint—came a fat and shabby *curé*. 'Well, better luck my friend,' Reggie murmured, left Dubois to pay the bill, and wandered away.

He met the *curé* by the church gate. Was it permitted to visit that interesting church? Certainly, it was permitted, but monsieur would find nothing of interest—it was new; it was, alas! a poor place.

The *curé* was right—it was new; it was garish, it was mean. He showed it to Reggie with an affecting simplicity of diffident pride, and Reggie was attentive. Reggie praised the care with which it was kept. 'You are kind, sir,' the *curé* beamed. 'You are just. In fact they are admirably pious, my poor people, but poor—poor.'

'You will permit the stranger—' Reggie slipped a note into his hand.

'Ah, monsieur! You are generous. It will be rewarded, please God.'

'It is nothing,' said Reggie quickly. 'Do not think of it.' They passed out of the church. 'I suppose this is almost the last place in France?'

'Sometimes I think we are forgotten,' the *curé* agreed. 'Yes, almost the last. Certainly we are all poor folk. There is only M. David, who is sometimes good to us.'

'A visitor?' Reggie said.

'Ah, no. He lives here. The Maison des Iles, you know. No? It is a school for young children—a school of luxury. He is a good man, M. David. Sometimes he will take, for almost a nothing, children who are weakly, and in a little while he has them as strong as the best. I have seen miracles. To be sure it is the best air in the world, here at Sarn. But he is a very good man. He calls his school 'of the islands' because of the islands out there'—the *curé* pointed to what looked like a reef of rocks. 'My poor people call them the islands of the blessed. It is not good religion, but they used to think the souls of the innocent went there. Yes, the Maison des Iles, his school is. But you should see it, sir. The children are charming.'

'If I had time—' said Reggie, and said good-bye.

Dubois was at the gate. Dubois took his arm and marched him off. 'My friend, almost thou persuadest me—' He spoke into Reggie's ear. 'Guess what I have found, will you? That motor-yacht, the yacht of M. David, she was away a week ten days ago.

And M. David on board. You see? It is possible she went over to England. A guess, yes, a chance, but one must avow it fits devilish well, if one can make it fit. A connection with all your fantasy—M. David over in England when Farquhar was drowned. Is it possible we arrive at last?'

'Yes, it could be. Guess what I've heard. M. David keeps school. That wasn't a bandstand. Open-air class-room. M. David is a very good man, and he uses his beautiful school to cure the children of the poor. He does miracles. The old *curé* has seen 'em.'

'The devil!' said Dubois. 'That does not fit at all. But a priest would see miracles. It is his trade.'

'Oh, no. No. Not unless they happen,' Reggie murmured.

'My friend, you believe more than any man I ever knew,' Dubois rumbled. 'Come, I must know more of this David. The sooner we were back at Quimper the better.'

'Yes. That is indicated. Quimper and telephone.' He checked a moment, and gazed anguish at Dubois. 'Oh, my hat, how I hate telephones.'

Dubois has not that old-fashioned weakness. Dubois, it is beyond doubt, enjoyed the last hours of that afternoon, shut into privacy at the post office with its best telephone, stirring up London and Paris and half France till sweat dripped from his big face and the veins of his brow dilated into knotted cords.

When he came into Reggie's room at the hotel it was already past dinner-time. Reggie lay on his bed, languid from a bath. 'My dear old thing,' he moaned sympathy. 'What a battle! You must have lost pounds.'

'So much the better,' Dubois chuckled. 'And also I have results. Listen. First. I praise the good Bell. He has it that a French boat—cutter rig with motor—was seen by fishermen in the bay off Lyncombe last week. They watched her, because they had suspicions she was poaching their lobsters and crabs, which they unaccountably believe is the habit of our honest French fishermen. She was lying in the bay the night of Tuesday—you see, the night that Farquhar disappeared. In the morning she was gone. They are not sure of the name, but they thought it was *Badboy*. That is near enough to Badebec, *hein*? In fact, myself, I do not understand the name Badebec.'

'Lady in Rabelais,' Reggie murmured. 'Rather interestin'. Shows the breadth of M. David's taste.'

'Aha. Very well. Here is a good deal for M. David to explain. Second, M. David himself. He is known: there is nothing against him. In fact he is like you, a man of science, a biologist, a doctor. He was brilliant as a student, which was about the same time that Farquhar studied art—and other things—in the Quartier Latin. David had no money. He served in hospitals for children; he set up his school here—a school for delicate children—four years ago. Its record is very good. He has medical inspection by a doctor from Quimper each month. But, third, Weber's nephew was at this school till July. He went home to Paris, they went out to Fontainebleau, and—piff!' Dubois snapped his fingers. 'He is dead like that. There is no doubt it was diphtheria. Do you say fulminating diphtheria? Yes, that is it.'

'I'd like a medical report,' Reggie murmured.

'I have asked for it. However—the doctors are above suspicion, my friend. And now, fourth—the Bernals are found. They are at Dijon. They have been asked what has become of their dear little boy, and, they reply, he is at school in Brittany. At the school of M. David, Maison des Iles, Quimper.'

'Yes. He would be. I see.'

'Name of a name! I think you have always seen everything.'

'Oh, no. No. Don't see it now,' Reggie mumbled. 'However. We're workin' it out. You've done wonderfully.'

'Not so bad.' Dubois smiled. 'My genius is for action.'

'Yes. Splendid. Yes. Mine isn't. I just went and had a look at the museum.'

'My dear friend,' Dubois condescended. 'Why not? After all, the affair is now for me.'

'Thanks, yes. Interestin' museum. Found a good man on the local legends there. Told me the Woman of Sarn used to have children sacrificed to her. That'll be what Farquhar had in his nice head. Though M. David is so good to children.'

'Aha. It explains, and it does not explain,' Dubois said. 'In spite of you, M. David remains an enigma. Let poor old Dubois try. I have all these people under observation—the Webers, the Bernals—they cannot escape me now. And there are good men gone out to watch over M. David in his Maison des Iles. Tomorrow we will go and talk to him, *hein*?'

'Pleasure,' Reggie murmured. 'You'd better go and have a bath now. You want it. And I want my dinner.' . . .

When they drove out to Sarn in the morning a second car followed them. In a blaze of hot sunshine they started, but they had not gone far before a mist of rain spread in from the sea, and by the time they reached the Maison des Iles they seemed to be in the clouds.

'An omen, *hein*?' Dubois made a grimace. 'At least it may be inconvenient—if he is alarmed; if he wishes to play tricks. We have no luck in this affair. But courage, my friend. Poor old Dubois, he is not without resource.'

Their car entered the walled enclosure of the Maison des Iles, the second stopped outside. When Dubois sent in his card to M. David, they were shown to a pleasant waiting-room, and had not long to wait.

David was dressed with a careless neatness. He was well groomed and perfectly at ease. His full red lips smiled; his dark eyes quizzed them. 'What a misery of a morning you have found, gentlemen. I apologise for my ocean. M. Dubois?' he made a bow.

'Of the Sûreté.' Dubois bowed. 'And M. Fortune, my distinguished *confrère* from England.'

David was enchanted. And what could he do for them?

'We make some little enquiries. First, you have here a boy— Tracy, the son of Mme Bernal. He is in good health?'

'Of the best.' David lifted his black brows. 'You will permit me to know why you ask.'

'Because another boy who was here is dead. The little nephew of M. Weber. You remember him?'

'Very well. He was a charming child. I regret infinitely. But you are without doubt aware that he fell ill on the holidays. It was a tragedy for his family. But the cause is not here. We have had no illness, no infection at all. I recommend you to Dr Lannion, at Quimper. He is our medical inspector.'

'Yes. So I've heard,' Reggie murmured. 'Have you had other cases of children who went home for the holidays and died?'

'It is an atrocious question!' David cried.

'But you are not quite sure of the answer?' said Dubois.

'If that is an insinuation, I protest,' David frowned. 'I have nothing to conceal, sir. It is impossible, that must be clear, I should know what has become of every child who has left my school. But, I tell you frankly, I do not recall any death but that of the little nephew of Weber, poor child.'

'Very well. Then you can have no objection that my assistant should examine your records,' said Dubois. He opened the window, and whistled and lifted a hand.

'Not the least in the world. I am at your orders.' David bowed. 'Permit me, I will go and get out the books,' and he went briskly.

'Now if we had luck he would try to run away,' Dubois rumbled. 'But do not expect it.'

'I didn't,' Reggie moaned.

And David did not run away. He came back and took them to his office, and there Dubois's man was set down to work at registers. 'You wish to assist?' David asked.

27

'No, thanks. No,' Reggie murmured. 'I'd like to loook at your school.'

'An inspection!' Dubois smiled. 'I shall be delighted. I dare to hope for the approval of a man of science so eminent.'

They inspected dormitories and dining-room and kitchen, class-rooms and workshop and laboratory. M. David was expansive and enthusiastic, yet modest. Either he was an accomplished actor, or he had a deep interest in school hygiene, and his arrangements were beyond suspicion. In the laboratory Reggie lingered. 'It is elementary,' David apologised. 'But what would you have? Some general science, that is all they can do, my little ones: botany for the most part; as you see, a trifle of chemistry to amuse them.'

'Yes. Quite sound. Yes. I'd like to see the other laboratory.'

'What?' David stared. 'There is only this.'

'Oh, no. Another one with a big microscope,' Reggie murmured. 'North side of the house.'

'Oh, la, la,' David laughed. 'you have paid some attention to my poor house. I am flattered. You mean my own den, where I play with marine biology still. Certainly you shall see it. But a little moment. I must get the key. You will understand. One must keep one's good microscope locked up. These imps, they play every-where.' He hurried out.

'*Bigre!* How the devil did you know there was another laboratory?' said Dubois.

'Name of a dog! Is there anything you do not see?' Dubois complained. 'Well, if we have any luck he has run away this time.'

They waited some long while, and Dubois's face was flattened against the window to peer through the rain at the man on watch. But David had not run away, he came back at last, and apologised for some delay with a fool of a master, heaven given him patience! He took them briskly to the other laboratory, his den.

It was not pretentious. There were some shelves of bottles, and a bench with a sink, and a glass cupboard which stood open and empty. On the broad table in the window was a microscope of high power, and some odds and ends.

Reggie glanced at the bottles of chemicals and came to the microscope. 'I play at what I worked at. That is middle age,' David smiled. 'Here is something a little interesting.' He slipped a slide into the microscope and invited Reggie to look.

'Oh, yes. One of the diatoms. Pretty one,' Reggie murmured, and was shown some more. 'Thanks very much.' A glance set Dubois in a hurry to go. David was affably disappointed. He had hoped they would lunch with him. The gentleman with the registers could hardly have finished his investigations. He desired an investigation the most complete.

'I will leave him here,' Dubois snapped, and they got away. 'Nothing, my friend?' Dubois muttered.

'No. That was the point,' Reggie said. ' "When they got there the cupboard was bare." '

As their car passed the gate, a man signalled to them out of the rain. They stopped just beyond sight of the house, and he joined them. 'Bouvier has held someone,' he panted. 'A man with a sack.' They got out of the car and Dubois waved him on.

Through the blinding rain-clouds they came to the back of the house, and, on the way up to the cliffs, found Bouvier with his hand on the collar of a sullen, stupefied Breton. A sack lay on the ground at their feet.

'He says it is only rubbish,' Bouvier said, 'and he was taking it to throw into the sea, where they throw their waste. But I kept him.'

'Good. Let us see.' Dubois pulled the sack open. 'The devil, it is nothing but broken glass!'

Reggie grasped the hand that was going to turn it over. 'No, you mustn't do that,' he said sharply. 'Risky.'

'Why? What then? It is broken glass and bits of jelly.'

'Yes. As you say. Broken glass and bits of jelly. However.' Over Reggie's wet face came a slow benign smile. 'Just what we wanted. Contents of cupboard which was bare. I'll have to do some work on this. I'm going to the hospital. You'd better collect David—in the other car. Good-bye.' . . .

Twenty-four hours, later, he came into a grim room of the *gendarmerie* at Quimper. There Dubois and David sat with a table between them, and neither man was a pleasant sight. David's florid colour was gone, he had become untidy, he sagged in his chair, unable to hide fatigue and pain. Dubois also was dishevelled, and his eyes had sunk and grown small, but the big face wore a look of hungry cruelty. He turned to Reggie. 'Aha. Here you are at last. And what do you tell M. David?'

'Well, we'll have a little demonstration.' Reggie set down a box on the table and took from it a microscope. 'Not such a fine instrument as yours, M. David, but it will do.' He adjusted a slide. 'You showed me some beautiful marine diatoms in your laboratory. Let me show you this. Also from your laboratory. From the sackful of stuff you tried to throw into the sea.'

David dragged himself up and looked, and stared at him, and dropped back in his chair.

'Oh, that's not all, no.' Reggie changed the slide. 'Try this one.'

Again, and more wearily, David looked. He sat down again. His full lips curled back to show his teeth in a grin. 'And then?' he said. 'What have you?' Dubois came to the microscope. 'Little chains of dots, eh?' Reggie put back the first slide. 'And rods with dots at the end.'

'Not bad for a layman, is it, M. David?' Reggie murmured. 'Streptococcus pyogenes, and the diphtheria bacillus. I've got some more—'

'Indeed?' David sneered.

'Oh, yes. But these will do. Pyogenes was found in poor little Weber: accountin' for the virulence of the diphtheria. Very efficient and scientific murder.'

'And the others?' Dubois thundered. 'The other children who went home for their holidays and died. Two, three, four, is it, David?'

David laughed. 'What does it matter? Yes, there are others who have gone to the isles of the blessed. But, also, there are many who have been made well and strong. I mock at you.'

'You have cause, Herod,' Dubois cried. 'You have grown rich on the murder of children. But it is we who laugh last. We deliver you to justice now.'

'Justice! Ah, yes, you believe that.' David laughed again. 'You are primitive, you are barbarous. Me, I am rational, I am a man of science. I sacrifice one life that a dozen may live well and happy. These who stand in the way of the rich, their deaths are paid for, and with the money I heal many. What, if life is valuable, is not this wisdom and justice? Let one die to save many—it is in all the religions, that. But no one believes his religions now. I—I believe in man. Well, I am before my time. But some day the world will be all Davids. With me it is finished.'

'Not yet, name of God!' Dubois growled.

'Oh yes, my friend. I am sick to death already. I have made sure of that.' He waved his hand at Reggie. 'You will not save me—no, not even you, my clever confrère. Good night! Go chase the Weber and the Bernal and the rest. David, he is gone into the infinite.' He fell back, a hand to his head.

Reggie went to him, and looked close and felt at him. 'Better take him away,' he pronounced. 'Hospital, under observation.'

Dubois gave the orders. . . . 'Play-acting, my friend,' he shrugged.

'Oh, no. No. That kind of man. Logical and drastic. He's ill all right. There was the diplococcus of meningitis in his collection. Might be that.' And it was. . . .

Ten days afterwards Dubois came to London with Reggie and gave Lomas a lecture on the case. 'I am desolated that I cannot offer you anyone to hang, my friend. But what can one do? The wretched Farquhar—I have no doubt he was murdered between David and Bernal. But there is no evidence. And, after all, David, he is dead, and we have Bernal for conspiracy to murder his stepson. That will do. It was, in fact, a case profoundly simple, like all the great crimes. To make a trade of arranging the deaths of unwanted children, that is very old. The distinction of David was to organise it scientifically, that is all. The child who was an heir to fortune, with a greedy one waiting to succeed, that was the child for him. Weber's nephew stood in the way of the beautiful Clotilde to Weber's fortune. Mrs Bernal's little boy was in the way of her second husband to the fortune of her father, the old millionaire. And the others! Well here is a beautiful modern school for delicate children, nine out of ten of them thrive marvellously. But, for the tenth, there is David's bacteriological laboratory, and a killing disease to take home with him when he goes for his holidays. Always at home, they die; always a disease of infection they could pick up anywhere. *Bigre!* It was a work of genius. And it would have gone on for ever but that this worthless Farquhar blunders into Brittany upon it, and begins to blackmail the beautiful Clotilde, the Bernal. Clotilde pays with her jewels, and has to pretend a robbery. Bernal will not pay—cannot, perhaps. Farquhar approaches the old grandfather, and Bernal calls in David, and the blackmailer is killed. The oldest story in the world. Rascals fall out, justice comes in. There is your angel of justice.' He bowed to Reggie. 'Dear master. You have shown me the way. Well, I am content to serve. Does he serve badly, poor old Dubois?'

'Oh, no. No. Brilliant,' Reggie murmured. 'Queer case, though. I believe David myself. He wanted to be a god. Make lives to his desire. And he did. Cured more than he killed. Far more. Then this fellow, who never wanted to be anything but a beast, blows in and beats him. Queer world. And David might have been a kindly, human fellow, if he hadn't had power. Dangerous stuff, science. Lots of us not fit for it.'